Roddy the Rooster

As a boy growing up on a hillside farm in southwest Missouri near Purdy, Eddie spent much of his time clearing new ground and raising strawberries. His parents taught him to be honest, work hard and treat people with respect. His interests include motivational speaking, inspirational teaching, and entertaining. For several years he has been a comedian on the Brumley music show in Branson, Missouri. He is also a song writer, musician and writer of inspirational and children's books.

Eddie and his wife, Evelyn, have four children and four grandchildren.

Eddie loves to tell stories of humor and common sense with practical applications for everyday life. He brings laughter and encouragement to readers and audiences of all ages.

Roddy the Rooster

By

Eddie Bowman

Illustrated by

Howard Prater

Ozark Publishing, Inc.
P.O. Box 228
Prairie Grove, AR 72753

Library of Congress cataloging-in-publication data

Bowman, Eddie, 1939-
    Roddy the rooster / by Eddie Bowman ;
    illustrated by Howard Prater.
        p.   cm.
    Summary: When the huge egg that had
    mysteriously appeared on the Smith's farm in
    the Ozarks hatches into the biggest chicken
    they have ever seen, Mr. and Mrs. Smith hope
    they won't have to worry about the chicken
    hawks anymore.
        ISBN 1-56763-326-9 (cloth). -- ISBN 1-56763-
327-7 (pbk.)
        [1. Chickens--Fiction. 2. Farm life--Ozark
Mountains--Fiction. 3. Ozark Mountains--Fiction.] I.
Prater, Howard, ill. II. Title. PZ7.B68345Ro
1998
[Fic}--dc21
                                    96-54301
                                        CIP
                                         AC

Printed in the United States of America

Contents

Chapter 1   The Big Surprise   1

Chapter 2   The Wait!   7

Chapter 3   Famous Protector   11

Chapter 4   What's in a Name?   17

Chapter 5   Pamela the Pullet   23

Chapter 6   Terror from the Sky   27

Chapter 7   Another Surprise!   35

Dedicated to

my grand-daughter Amy Gayle Gould

Chapter 1

The Big Surprise

Mr. and Mrs. Smith lived on a little farm nestled back in the hills of the Ozarks. Many happy years had passed since they had met. They raised five children, three boys and two girls. When the children grew up and married, they moved away. But Mr. and Mrs. Smith stayed on their little farm, enjoying the way of life they had known for so long.

They always raised a big garden and had some fruit trees. This gave them many fruits and vegetables to eat. When winters came, their cellar always contained a good supply of canned goods to last them through the cold days ahead.

They had two horses that Mr. Smith used to plow the garden and

cultivate his crops. They had a cow that provided milk, cream, and butter, and they had some chickens that laid eggs. Sometimes Mrs. Smith would gather as many as twenty eggs or more a day. So they always had fresh eggs to eat and even had some to sell to neighbors.

Mr. Smith had cut some oak saw logs and hauled them to the sawmill. He built a chicken house with the oak lumber. He also made a few nests and filled them with straw for the chickens so they would have a nice place to lay their eggs.

Mrs. Smith loved her chickens, and on this pretty spring evening while Mr. Smith was milking the cow, she went to the corncrib for a few ears of corn. She shelled the corn and scattered it on the ground in the chicken yard, calling, "Chick, chick, chick!" The hungry chickens all came running, gobbling down the corn. Then she searched the nests and found nineteen eggs! She placed them in her basket.

As she was leaving, she noticed a very large egg lying by itself near the gate of the chicken yard. "How strange," she thought as she stooped down to pick it up. She was certain it was not there when she entered the gate a few minutes earlier or she would have seen it. But there was no question,

it was there now, all right. She showed
it to Mr. Smith.

He said, "That's the largest egg I've ever seen! Why don't we put it under Hester, the settin' hen, that started settin' today? We'll see what hatches out."

So, Mrs. Smith put the large egg beneath Hester, along with the ten other eggs already there, and they waited for the eggs to hatch.

Chapter 2

The Wait!

It takes twenty-one days for chickens to hatch. That gave Mr. and Mrs. Smith plenty of time to get ready for the new chicks. They went to the feed store in town and bought a sack of mash. They repaired the fence around the chicken yard and made some repairs on the chicken house. They fixed up a little coop to give the chicks some extra care when they hatched. But it sure was hard to protect them from wild animals. One of the worse-feared enemies was the red-tailed chicken hawk. Mr. Smith had tried to shoot the hawk, but the hawk had outsmarted him. One of their young hens had been carried off by the hawk on the day before they had found the large egg. The hawk had not been seen since, but Mr. Smith knew he would be back.

Mrs. Smith fed and watered the chickens every day, but she gave special attention to Hester, the settin' hen. It would not be long, now, before the eggs would begin to hatch.

On Friday evening, Mrs. Smith did her usual chores, then as darkness began to fall, she stepped inside the chicken house. The chickens had all gone to roost. Hester was quietly sitting on her eggs. Mrs. Smith said,

"Hester, tomorrow your little chicks should hatch. I'll see you the first thing in the morning. And, by the way, you be sure that big egg hatches! I can't wait to see what it will be!" Mrs. Smith shut the door to the chicken house, latched it, and went to

the house. Mr. Smith had just fin-
ished his chores and was sitting at the
kitchen table when she walked in.
She said, "Well, tomorrow is the big
day! Tomorrow we will have some
new chicks!"

"Yes," said Mr. Smith, "and
tomorrow we should know the mystery of the big egg!"

Chapter 3

Famous Protector

On Saturday morning, Mrs. Smith was awakened by the crowing of the roosters. As soon as she was dressed, she went to the chicken house. She moved near Hester's nest, but she could see there were no new chicks yet. I'll just have to wait a while, she thought as she went back to the house to prepare breakfast.

Breakfast was the most important meal to Mr. and Mrs. Smith. They worked hard on the farm and needed the energy a good breakfast could provide. Ham and eggs with gravy and biscuits was a typical morning meal. And they usually had some blackberry jelly and butter with their biscuits. Often, Mrs. Smith would open a quart of canned straw-berries. They were delicious poured over biscuits and topped with cream from the Jersey cow.

After they had eaten, Mrs. Smith washed the dishes, then went back to the chicken house. She was feeding corn to the chickens when she heard the peep, peep of little chicks! She went inside the chicken house to see! As Mrs. Smith came closer to Hester, she heard several more "peep, peeps."

Then she heard something that startled her! It was not the high-pitched "peep, peep" that baby chicks normally make, but a strange, harsh, and throaty **peep, peep!** What on earth could be making such a sound?

Then, she could hardly believe her eyes! She was looking at the biggest yellow chick she had ever seen! It was two or three times as large as any of the others! And not only was it an unusually large chick, but it had a look in its eyes Mrs. Smith had never seen in a chicken! It was like, "Here I am, your protector! Just feed me plenty of corn, and I will protect the chicken yard!" Then a name came to Mrs. Smith. Rodmond! It was an old German name that meant famous protector! "I'll call him Roddy for short," she said to herself.

Then Mr. Smith came in to see the new chicks. He was amazed at the size of the big one! "What are you going to name him?" he asked.

She said, "I've already named him. His name is Roddy."

"Why Roddy?" asked Mr. Smith.

Mrs. Smith replied, "Because the name means protector. I believe Roddy's mission is to protect the chicken yard. When he becomes grown, he will be a giant! Then maybe the chicken hawks and other chicken killers will leave our chickens alone."

"Sounds good," said Mr. Smith. "He's almost a giant already! And the way we've been losing chickens, they sure need a good protector. Just maybe that's Roddy's purpose, to guard the chicken yard. Yes, I believe he will be a guardian rooster. I just hope he doesn't step on his brothers and sisters!"

Chapter 4

What's in a Name?

Roddy was so large that Mrs. Smith didn't want to put him in the small coop with the rest, being afraid he might hurt them. And since all the chicks seemed to be so fond of Roddy, Mrs. Smith just turned them out into the chicken yard. Roddy ate the mash that was given to him, then he ate corn right along with the adult chickens. Mrs. Smith had never seen a baby chick eat like a grown-up chicken. And how he grew!

The baby chicks began to venture out a little further from their mother each day and explore their new world. If they became scared, they would come running to their mother to take cover beneath her out-spread wings. One day they got scared when they saw a mouse. Roddy came running as fast as he could to his mother. He ran right into her and knocked her down!

"SQUEAK!"

So, Hester had a good talk with her growing son. She said, "Roddy, you are too big to run from every little frightening thing you see. You're bigger than I am! And it's time for you to start standing your ground when danger comes. You need to believe in yourself. Remember your name and who you are! You are our protector, so live up to your name!"

From then on, Roddy never ran from danger. Roddy grew up to be so brave and strong, he could defeat any enemy that dared to attack. More than once, he saved the chickens from some wild animal. But so far, he had not had an encounter with a chicken hawk. His mother had told him that chicken hawks were especially dangerous and very sneaky.

Roddy ate more corn every day and began doing chicken exercises. Four or five chickens would crawl on Roddy's back, and he would do squats. Then he would spread his

wings over the edges of two chicken coops and lift himself and let himself down one hundred clucks a day. He got so strong that he almost scared himself!

Mrs. Smith was beginning to get worried because the corn was nearly gone from the corncrib. But Mr. Smith said, "Don't worry. Tomorrow, we'll hitch the horses to the wagon and go out and gather corn. We have a good crop this year and it is time to be harvested."

This made Mrs. Smith feel really good and it really pleased Roddy and the chickens, for they all knew that even if the winter were long and cold, there would be plenty to eat.

Chapter 5

Pamela the Pullet

It did turn out to be a long, cold winter, but for Roddy, it didn't matter. He had plenty to eat, and he stayed nice and warm inside the chicken house. But there was something else. He had a wonderful warm feeling inside himself he had never had before. Roddy was falling in love!

A few weeks earlier, a neighbor had a farm sale, and Mrs. Smith had bought six young pullets (females) to go with her other chickens. It was one of these young pullets named

Pamela that nearly took Roddy's breath away! Roddy thought she was the prettiest chicken in the world!

They would often go some-where and talk for hours. Mrs. Smith couldn't help but notice how much time they spent together and how Roddy always made sure Pamela got all the corn she wanted. And, my, how he protected her! If danger approached, he would raise his huge wing and hide Pamela until the dan-ger had passed.

Because they had such love for each other, the long winter passed for them like it was no time at all. Then came the warm sunshine of spring.

Chapter 6

Terror from the Sky

It was about two-thirty in the afternoon on a Thursday in May when the dreaded chicken hawk decided to visit the Smith farm. Mr. Smith and his team of horses were plowing in the bottom just across Polk Creek. Mrs. Smith had gone into town with a neighbor to buy some sugar, thread, some plow points for Mr. Smith, and a few other things they needed. So no one was home when the chicken hawk struck!

It was a lovely day. A few clouds floated overhead in a beautiful blue sky. Roddy and Pamela were engaged in a dreamy-eyed conversation, making plans for their wedding which was coming up very soon. A hen was cackling because she had just laid an egg. Somewhere in the distance, a dog barked, but the chickens showed no alarm. They felt perfectly secure in the safety of the chicken yard, especially with Roddy around.

Meanwhile, the chicken hawk had been gliding lazily in the sky, waiting for his opportunity. If he could get rid of Roddy, he knew it would be easy to get all the rest.

Then it happened! There was no warning! The hawk came swooping

down at lightning speed and hit Roddy right behind the neck!

The impact was deadening! Roddy was temporarily paralyzed!

He tried to raise his strong wings, but they would not move! He was almost unconscious.

The chickens were all scared to death and watched helplessly as the chicken hawk lifted Roddy into the air and flew off with him. Pamela was terrified! She could not bear to think of something happening to her Roddy!

"Oh, Roddy!" she called as the chicken hawk flew away. "You know I will always love you! Please, Roddy, don't let the chicken hawk kill you! Save us, Roddy! I love you!'

Mr. Smith had stopped his team to give them a few minutes' rest while he sat down beneath a big oak tree. He reached for his half-gallon fruit jar. It was wrapped in burlap and filled with cold water from the spring. As he tipped the jar to drink, his eye caught a glimpse of the chicken hawk setting Roddy down in the clover field to finish him off.

But the flight had revived Roddy! He had new life! And not only that, but the words of Pamela were burning in his heart, "I love you!" He also recalled the words of his mother, "Live up to your name!"

Mr. Smith rose up, hurried to the fence row, and watched through some sassafras trees at what was happening. When the hawk set Roddy down, Mr. Smith said he had never seen such a fight! Feathers, dirt, and clover flew everywhere!

And what was so amazing, said Mr. Smith later, was that not only did that rooster whip that chicken hawk, but he made him fly him back across

Polk Creek and set him gently down
into the chicken yard!

Mrs. Smith was just returning
from town when she saw it. She said,
"Now I've seen everything!"

Pamela ran out to meet Roddy. He wrapped a big wing around her. All the chickens were thrilled! The chicken hawk, with his feathers all drooping, quietly disappeared. Famous protector—Roddy had lived up to his name!

Chapter 7

Another Surprise!

A few days later, Mr. and Mrs. Smith were sitting in the porch swing talking when they heard the swish, swish of wings. They looked up, and the sky was filled with chicken hawks!

"Oh, no!" shouted Mr. Smith, as he started for his shotgun. "All these hawks have come in vengeance! They will kill all our chickens!"

"Wait!" hollered Mrs. Smith. "They're not here to harm the chickens! Look! Roddy and Pamela have just gotten married!"

Then Pamela crawled onto Roddy's back. He flapped his huge wings, and they were airborne! Roddy had learned that he could fly like an eagle! The newlyweds were

being escorted away by the chicken hawks, with the red-tailed hawk leading the way!

Roddy and Pamela were never seen again. To this day, no one knows for sure the answer to this mystery! Where did they go? Did Roddy take Pamela to some home in the sky, perhaps where he had come from?

We may never know. But we do know one thing. Mr. and Mrs. Smith said that chicken hawks never bothered their chickens again. One morning, however, Mrs. Smith went to the chicken house and discovered that a weasel had come and killed two chickens. But the very next morning, she found another large egg lying by itself near the gate of the chicken yard. It was in the exact spot the first large egg had been. Mrs. Smith smiled as she carefully picked up the large egg and placed it underneath the settin' hen.